# CRUSHED BY A CRUSH

*To everything there is a season, a time for every purpose under Heaven*

*Ecclesiastes 3:1 NKJV*

## Taiwo Iredele Odubiyi

# DEDICATION

To God

And

To every teenage boy and girl holding on to their faith in a world that doesn't always make it easy.

*I pray that your strength is renewed as you draw from the power of God's Word and the depth of His love, in Jesus' name.*

# CONTENT

# CHAPTER 1

## Torn Between Two Worlds

Janet, fifteen, was a secondary school student with one year to go. She was the kind of girl people described as quiet, thoughtful, well-behaved, and a good Christian. In public, she rarely drew attention to herself and opened up only when she felt truly safe. Among close friends and family, however, she could be surprisingly expressive. When amused, her bright, high-pitched laughter would ring out—whether in the classroom, church, or at home.

As the youngest in a lively household of five children, she had grown up in a world full of voices. She was used to constant noise, overlapping conversations, shared meals, and the occasional sibling quarrel.

Alongside the noise, she was also used to structure and early morning family prayers which was usually led by her father. Every weekday morning at 5:30 sharp, her father's firm voice would sound through the rented three-bedroom apartment in which the family lived, calling everyone to the living room for family devotion. The man, an accountant by profession, served as an assistant pastor at The Vine Worship Center, a small but thriving church in their neighborhood where the family worshipped. Janet's mother was a deaconess in the same church and in charge of the children's department.

Janet had three older brothers and a sister. Two of the brothers were twins. They studied English at a university and were currently away in another state for their NYSC service year, which was a one-year mandatory national service program for Nigerian university graduates. Her third brother and her sister were in different Universities, studying Pharmacy and Accounting, respectively. Both lived on campus, leaving Janet as the only one still living at home with their parents. She hoped to become a medical doctor.

Janet carried herself with a gentle grace—a reflection of the Christian values instilled in her from childhood. She had given her life to Jesus at the age of seven during a children's service at church, and she could still remember the moment clearly. That day, her heart had felt like it was burning as she made a firm decision to follow Jesus and to know God more.

Singing in the children's choir quickly followed because she loved to sing and had a beautiful, strong, and pure voice. Now, she was a member of the teens' choir.

In Elementary school, being a Christian was simpler because her peers were mostly innocent and life was less demanding. Since stepping into the complex world of High School, however, Janet had found it increasingly hard to remain consistent in her walk with God. The expectations were different now. There was a pull—subtle but strong—to fit in, to be seen, and liked by her classmates. And although she never dropped her Christian faith, she could feel the quiet war going on inside of her: the desire to obey God versus the longing to belong and relax her standards.

She attended the school's fellowship which held every Friday afternoon in the school hall, right after classes ended and closing bell rang. Occasionally, she was asked to lead the congregation of about fifty students and a handful of teachers, in praise and worship.

Among her peers, she was known to be a good Christian. Yet, beneath the surface, she knew something was shifting. Lately, her convictions didn't feel as firm. The struggle wasn't with what she believed, but with what she was seeing. Some of the very students who claimed to be Christians—those who stood beside her in the school fellowship with hands lifted up in worship—lived in ways that contradicted everything she had been taught. They did things she believed were sinful, yet they were confident, outspoken, and popular—seemingly unbothered by the double lives that they led.

Janet knew their behavior was wrong, and yet … a part of her admired them. She admired their boldness, the way they talked, and behaved in school. They had a kind of freedom that made her feel like she was missing out. Soon, she found herself silently making comparisons and wondering if her quiet obedience still mattered as much as it used to.

Janet had a few friends in the school, but three girls had become particularly close to her over the years—Aanu, Lizzy, and Ada. It hadn't started that way though. Back in their first year, she had been wary of the girls. They claimed to be Christians and attended the school fellowship every Friday, but their actions didn't always reflect what they professed. There was something about their laughter and the way they talked about boys, that made Janet keep her distance.

But by their second year, things had changed. Janet and the three girls began to talk and share experiences, and now, they were her inner circle. They were classmates, but not in the same class. They understood each other, they laughed at the same jokes, and knew each other's secrets.

Aanu was the liveliest of them all, and she had a boyfriend who was in the final year in the school. The sixteen-year-old boy wasn't a Christian, but that fact did not bother Aanu. She spoke about him often—how charming he was, how he made her laugh, and how she sometimes had to come up with clever stories to keep her parents from knowing that she had a boyfriend.

Lizzy wasn't much different. Her boyfriend was older, worked at a post office nearby, and was waiting for university admission. She spoke of him to her friends with dreamy eyes and pride.

Only Janet and Ada were not in a relationship, but with the kind of stories they heard from Aanu and Lizzy—about the gifts, the attention, and the phone calls at night from their boyfriends … it was hard for them not to imagine what having a boyfriend would be like. Though they had not said it out loud, Janet knew that both she and Ada were hoping they'd soon have their own stories too.

The four girls walked to and from school side by side, although there were days that Aanu did not go with them, but with her boyfriend.

Then came Michael.

He was in the same grade as Janet and her friends, but in a different class. His class was just two doors away from Janet's class. While she was taking science subjects—Physics, Chemistry, Biology—Michael was an arts student and he had a natural gift for drawing and painting.

He was known across the school not just as an artist but as an athlete too. He ran the 100 and 200-meter races and almost always won.

He was tall, talented, and confident … qualities that drew Janet's eyes more often than she liked to admit. She noticed him during morning assemblies, at school events, and sometimes in the corridors between classes.

At first, it had been a simple admiration. Then she began to notice small things about him—the way he smiled, the way he talked, and the way he walked. Soon, thoughts of him would slip into her mind and stay there.

 # CHAPTER 2

## Janet's Confession

On the first Monday of February, when the closing bell rang, Janet carried her school bag, went to her friends' classes, and soon, they were ready to leave.

When they reached the school gate, Janet saw Michael near the gate, talking and laughing with two of his classmates.

*He's so handsome!* she thought.

Suddenly, he looked in her direction and when their eyes met, her heart skipped a beat.

He seemed to look at her a little longer than necessary before he turned back to his friends.

Janet told herself that she had to tell her three friends about her growing feelings for Michael now. She knew they would laugh, but she could no longer keep this to herself. She'd like to hear their opinion on what she could do about it.

The four girls walked past the boys and through the gate. As soon as they were outside, Janet glanced back to be sure no student was close enough to overhear what she was about to say. Then she announced to her friends that she had something to say, and then she finally let the words tumble out. She told them about Michael: how she liked him, and how she hadn't been able to stop thinking about him.

It happened just as Janet expected. Laughter bounced through the dusty road as Aanu, half in shock and half in delight, gave her a lighthearted smack on the back. Their reactions were loud, teasing, and full of excitement, the way only close friends could be. And though Janet tried to act embarrassed, a part of her was relieved. The secret was out.

The voices of nearby students drifted in the air, but the four girls barely noticed as they were too caught up in their discussion.

"When did you start feeling this way?" Ada asked, curious.

Janet hesitated for a moment as she thought about it, then she exhaled and said, "About three weeks ago. It just...crept in. I didn't even notice at first."

"Wow!" Ada exclaimed.

"I don't know what to do." Janet confessed, her voice low and uncertain.

"You do know there's no harm in talking to him, right?" Aanu said immediately, nudging her lightly on the arm.

Janet blinked. "Talk to him?!" She gave Aanu a wide-eyed look. "Are you serious?"

"Yes, I'm serious. It wouldn't hurt to at least get to know him if you've been obsessing quietly for about three weeks now."

"I don't know if I want to do that." Janet looked thoughtful and doubtful. "I don't even think he's a Christian. I mean, he doesn't attend fellowship meetings."

Aanu scoffed. "Girl, you act like you don't know my story! My boyfriend's not a Christian either, but we're cool. We like each other, and we're fine."

Janet sighed heavily. "Ah! I really like Michael. If only he had a relationship with God!" She let out a frustrated sound and shook her head.

"You can convert him if that matters to you." Lizzy suggested.

Janet quickly shook her head. "No, Lizzy. No one can convert another person. That's not how it works. Only God can do that."

"True," It was Aanu who replied, "but we can influence them. Sometimes, people need a push to think differently."

"But I don't think you've been able to influence your boyfriend … going by the things you've been telling us." Janet told her.

"I know; that boy can be stubborn." Aanu admitted. They laughed.

"Aanu, my thinking is this … even if Michael is a Christian," Ada interjected gently, "have you thought about the fact that he might not like Janet the same way?"

"And let's not forget," Lizzy added, raising an eyebrow, "Michael is popular. Really popular. How do we know he doesn't already have a girlfriend?"

The others nodded slightly as they considered the possibilities.

"Well, Janet, I could talk to him for you." Aanu offered.

Janet's head jerked back as if stung by a bee. "To tell him? No! No way! Don't do that!"

"Why not?" Aanu asked and laughed. "You never know … he might like you."

They continued tossing ideas and opinions back and forth, their voices rising and falling, sometimes in amusement, sometimes in concern.

Janet appreciated her friends' support, their playful jabs, and their serious advice.

Yet beneath it all, she felt a warning in her heart. A still, small voice that whispered that this wasn't right … just like some other things in her life lately.

She also sensed a voice urging her to speak with someone older; someone who knew God and could offer wise, godly counsel on how she should handle her feelings. Yet, the thought of having a boyfriend thrilled her, and she felt confident she could navigate it on her own, especially with her friends' support.

Suddenly, a voice called out from behind them. "Janet!"

Janet turned and saw Chioma walking briskly toward them, waving slightly.

"This girl again!" Lizzy muttered under her breath.

Aanu rolled her eyes. "Here comes the preacher."

Ada and Lizzy hissed, but Janet smiled, even if it was a little guarded. She liked Chioma, but her friends didn't.

Chioma was also a Christian, but Janet's three friends thought that she was too uptight, and too judgmental, especially when she pointed out things they did that she believed were wrong. And because they kept their distance from Chioma, Janet had started to do the same. Not completely, but just enough to keep the peace.

However, Chioma, who was Janet's church member, still tried to be close to Janet. They were both in the teens choir at church, and they sang together in the school fellowship too. That bond hadn't broken yet.

Chioma finally caught up, slightly out of breath. "I've been calling you since. What were you all talking about that you didn't even hear me?"

The others stayed quiet; their expressions unreadable.

Janet answered quickly, "We were just talking. Nothing much."

Chioma glanced around at the faces, noting the silence. She looked like she wanted to ask more, but held back.

Janet could already guess what Chioma would say if she knew what they'd been discussing. She would think that Janet was backsliding; after all, Chioma didn't even believe that Aanu was truly born again.

As Chioma stood there next to her, Janet felt torn between the voices of her three friends and another voice that seemed deeper; more certain. And she knew she couldn't ignore this voice forever.

The five girls continued walking.

Soon, Ada slowed her pace as they approached a junction. "This is my turn." She said, adjusting the strap of her bag. "I'll see you all tomorrow."

"Alright, Ada. Bye!" Aanu waved.

"Later, Ada!" Lizzy called.

Janet and Chioma waved and said good night.

"Good night." Ada said, and with one last look, she disappeared into the street leading to her house.

Janet and the others walked a little further before they each split off as well.

Eventually, Janet found herself alone as she approached her gate. The street was quiet, except for the barking of a dog and the hum of generators from three houses on the street. The sound signaled that the electricity had gone out. Her parents owned a generator too, but they would not be at home at the moment. Her parents had gone to work and usually returned home around 7pm. The generator would be turned on if the electricity was still out when they returned.

 # CHAPTER 3

## A Secret Shared

Janet arrived at the cream and gray painted house, and when she pushed open the black pedestrian gate, its hinges creaked slightly as it swung inward. She stepped into the compound of the aging two-story structure with concrete flooring.

Her family lived in the three-bedroom apartment at the rear of the second floor. The staircase, tucked to the left side of the building, had iron railing and slightly cracked concrete steps. As she climbed the staircase, her school shoes tapped against the concrete, until she reached the door of their apartment.

She slipped off her backpack and fished out the house key from a small inner pocket. After fitting it into the lock and giving it a slight jiggle, the door clicked open. She stepped inside, closed it behind her, and locked it.

The apartment smelled faintly of the stockfish that her mother bought from a store yesterday and left on the kitchen shelf. The living room was modestly furnished. It had three sofas with slightly faded upholstery, a center table with a glass top, and a wooden shelf that was crowded with books and framed photographs, among other things.

She dropped her backpack on the tiled floor of the living room and made her way to her bedroom. The room had two narrow beds placed on opposite sides of the room, separated by a small wooden table. She and her sister, Flourish, used to share the space before Flourish gained admission to the university last year. Now, the room was mostly hers, except during the holidays when Flourish returned.

The walls were painted gray, with one side decorated with photographs, stickers, and posters of Bible verses and inspirational quotes. A small wardrobe stood in the corner beside the window, and there was a standing fan by the door.

Her parents occupied the largest bedroom, while her three brothers shared the third room, which was slightly more spacious than the one that she and her sister shared.

Just as she was about to open the windows of the room, the light of the room came on, which meant that electricity had returned. Janet quickly changed out of her white and brown school uniform into a comfortable house dress.

Hanging her uniform, she returned to the living room, opened the windows, and turned the ceiling fan on. Then she headed to the kitchen with her stomach grumbling quietly.

Opening the refrigerator and checking the covered bowls in it, she found some boiled yam, leftover stew and a piece of fish. She combined the items in a bowl, then opened the microwave to heat the food. A few minutes later, she returned to the living room with a steaming bowl of food and a cup of cold water in hand. Settling into the couch, she began to eat.

About twenty minutes later, she had finished eating. Taking her dishes to the kitchen, she washed them thoroughly and wiped the counter clean. Back in the living room, she opened her backpack and brought out her notebooks and textbooks. She spread them across the table and began working on her assignments.

By the time the wall clock chimed six, she was done. She stretched, and as she began packing up her books, a small smile played on her lips. There was no church service today—it was Monday—and that meant she could relax for the rest of the evening.

Shortly after, she turned the TV on, stretched out on the three-seater sofa in the living room, and rested her head on one of the armrests.

Though her body was resting, her mind refused to rest; once again drifting back to Michael just as it had been doing for the past three weeks. As she thought about him, she barely registered the scenes flickering across the TV screen.

*Michael*, she thought, her gaze moving from the TV to the ceiling above. Three whole weeks, and the feelings had not gone away. She turned onto her side, then onto her back again, adjusting her position, but all that didn't help to calm the thoughts swirling in her head.

*Why can't I stop thinking about him? Is this love?!*

Then her mind went to her discussion with her friends about Michael, and she wondered if she should take Aanu's advice.

Her thoughts turned to her sister, Flourish. Though she and Flourish were close and spoke often on the phone, Janet hadn't mentioned anything about

Michael. She already knew how Flourish would react; there was no way Flourish would approve of what Janet was considering.

She shook her head as she thought … *Flourish wouldn't understand. She'd just say, "You're too young, Janet." Just like Mom and Dad would. They'd all look at me like I've done something wrong just for having these feelings.*

It wasn't as if she planned for it to happen. Michael had just … caught her attention. And now, it had become something more.

*What should I do?* The question came again. *Should I follow Aanu's advice? Or maybe talk to Flourish after all?*

No answer came. She heard only the low chatter of the TV characters, and the sound of the fan spinning above her. The questions remained in her heart, unanswered.

*********

It was a week later, on a Tuesday afternoon during lunch break. Some students were seated at their desks, eating and talking in clusters, while others leaned against the windows or lounged in corners, enjoying the midday lull.

Janet was seated near the back of the classroom, reading a book as she ate her food.

Ada entered, walking quickly with a determined look on her face. Her eyes scanned the room until they landed on Janet. "Janet!"

Janet looked up, a spoon of rice halfway to her mouth.

"Come!" Ada said firmly, motioning with her hand.

Janet was surprised. "Now?"

Ada nodded. "Yes. It's urgent."

Without asking further questions, Janet dropped her spoon into her bowl, stood up, and followed her out of the classroom, still clutching the bowl of food.

They stepped out into the corridor where the noise of the classroom faded behind them. The hall was quiet except for a few students walking lazily down the passage. Ada led her to a corner by a staircase, where they were mostly out of sight.

"What's going on?" Janet asked, her voice low.

Ada glanced around, then leaned in close. "I think Michael knows."

Janet blinked, confused. "Knows what?"

"That you like him."

Janet's heart jolted. She stared at Ada as if she hadn't heard right. "What?! Michael knows?! How?! When?! Who told him?!"

Ada crossed her arms and shook her head. "I don't know exactly, but Tunde—the one in my class—came to me just now and said he heard that you like Michael. According to him, Michael already knows."

Janet's mouth fell slightly open and her face changed. The bowl in her hand suddenly felt heavy as her mind began to race. "But ... how?! I didn't say anything to anyone. Only you, Aanu, and Lizzy knew."

"I know." Ada said, shrugging. "I was surprised when Tunde told me."

Janet looked away, her mind racing. *Could Lizzy have said something? Or Aanu? Maybe someone overheard us talking?* She couldn't think straight. "Have you told Aanu and Lizzy?"

Ada shook her head. Then she said, "I wonder if Michael will call you to ask you about it."

"I hope not. I don't even want him to see me right now."

They stood in silence for a moment.

"We'll talk more after school … on our way home."
Janet said finally.

Ada nodded. "Yeah, but try not to panic. Okay?"

Janet forced a small nod, already feeling uneasy.
Lunch break was only halfway through, but suddenly,
she had no appetite left at all.

 # CHAPTER 4

## When Secrets Spill

Later that afternoon, the final bell rang, echoing through the school compound. As students began to pour out of classrooms, their chatter filled the air.

Janet immediately carried her bag, left her classroom, and walked toward the school gate to wait for her friends. Soon, they came, and they began the familiar walk home along the dusty roadside.

Aanu chatted lightly at first, about a funny moment in her class. Ada and Lizzy laughed, but Janet was quiet, distracted.

When there was a pause, Janet slowed her pace and turned to face them, her expression serious. "Okay. I need to say something." She said, stopping on the sidewalk.

The other girls stopped and turned toward her.

She went on. "Ada told me something during lunch today … something I didn't expect to hear."

Aanu and Lizzy had a curious expression on their faces as they asked, "What did she say?"

"She said Michael knows that I like him."

Lizzy's eyes widened. Aanu blinked. Ada looked at the others, arms crossed, silently confirming the statement.

Janet's voice hardened. "I need to know … who talked? Because I only told you three!"

There was a pause. An awkward silence hung over the group for a moment, broken only by the sound of passing vehicles and voices of students walking by.

Aanu shifted on her feet slightly, and then let out a breath. "Okay," she said slowly. "I might have … mentioned it to my boyfriend."

Janet's head snapped toward her. "You what?!"

"I didn't mean to!" Aanu said quickly, holding her hands up defensively. "It just came up. We were talking about people in school and somehow it slipped. I honestly didn't think he'd say anything to anyone."

"Well, clearly he did." Janet said, her voice rising. She folded her arms tightly. "Now it's out. And Michael knows. How am I supposed to face him?"

Ada frowned and glanced at Aanu. "You should've told us that you said something."

"I know." Aanu mumbled. "I'm really sorry, Janet."

"Well, it's not the end of the world." Lizzy said with a half-smile, trying to lighten the mood.

Janet gave her a look, unimpressed. "That's easy for you to say. You're not the one who feels like she's been exposed."

"I didn't mean to betray your trust." Aanu said. "But maybe it's not all bad. Now that he knows … he might actually say something, make a move. Let's just wait and see."

Janet didn't respond as she looked ahead, eyes squinting slightly at the path before them. Her thoughts were already swirling with worry … and curiosity.

What if Michael had been thinking about her too?

Or worse … what if he laughed it off with his friends? Her stomach twisted at the thought.

"I just … I'm not sure that I know how to handle this." She confessed.

The girls walked on in silence for a few seconds.

Then Lizzy nudged her gently. "Well, if he decides to talk to you, don't faint." She teased.

Janet couldn't help the small smile that tugged at her lips. But deep down, her heart was caught in a tug-of-war between embarrassment, a flicker of hope, and concern that something about it all was wrong.

**********

That Tuesday afternoon, Michael had to see the sports teacher, and when the closing bell rang, he went over. The teacher was talking with the school Principal, and Michael decided to wait. He stood in the corridor, by the door of the teacher's office, leaning one shoulder against the wall. His backpack hung from his left shoulder, the strap tugging slightly at his collar, and his arms were folded in a loose, almost distracted manner across his chest.

His eyes followed the movement of students as they now trickled out of the school compound but he wasn't really watching them.

His gaze was distant and unfocused. He was still thinking about what Daniel—his friend in the final year—had said to him yesterday. Shifting his weight from one leg to another, he replayed the conversation in his head.

"So, apparently, that Janet girl likes you." Daniel had said with a smirk, nudging him in the side.

Michael had blinked, surprised. "Janet? Which Janet?"

Daniel described her.

"Oh, that girl?"

Daniel nodded, clearly enjoying the conversation. "Yes. Heard it from someone who heard it from Aanu's boyfriend. Word's been going around."

Michael had chuckled then, more amused than flattered. He hadn't seen that coming at all. Didn't Janet claim to be a Christian?! He wondered, surprised.

Now, standing by the corridor, he let the news roll around in his head again.

Janet. He pictured her … always neat; always quiet. The kind of girl who kept to herself, answered questions in class without showing off, and always attended the school fellowship. She wasn't like the girls who flirted or chased attention.

"Wow!" He muttered under his breath, with a half-smile.

She was a nice girl, and he liked the fact that she liked him, but the truth was … he wasn't interested.

She wasn't the kind of girl he saw himself with. She was a Christian, he wasn't. Besides, she was too quiet for his liking. He liked bold girls. Girls who didn't overthink every little thing. Janet was...too serious. Too reserved. His friends would be shocked if they saw him with her.

Still, the news was kind of funny.

# CHAPTER 5

## The Letter

That week, whenever Janet passed by Michael in the hallway or saw him across the schoolyard, he acted like nothing had changed. No glances. No smiles. No tension. Just Michael—confident and slightly aloof, with a facial expression that was sometimes unreadable.

By Tuesday of the following week, Janet had managed to shove the situation into the back of her mind as she had two tests coming up the following Wednesday that she had to prepare for.

During lunch break, she told her three friends that she wouldn't be going home immediately after school because she needed to go to the school library to get some books for her revision.

When the final bell eventually rang that afternoon, Janet made her way to the school library, which was quieter than usual. It took her about twenty minutes to get the books, and she checked them out at the front desk.

As she stepped out of the building and passed through the school gate, her mind was already on the things she would need to do at home—her school assignment, go to church for choir rehearsal, and study when she returned home before bed.

"Janet!" A voice called from across the road.

She paused mid-step, and turned her head. It was Chuks, one of the boys in Michael's class. He was standing on the opposite side of the road, waving.

"Wait! I have something for you!" He called again.

Janet stopped and waited for him to cross the road. What could Chuks want with her?

He crossed and came to her, smiling. "I was looking for you when the school closed but didn't see you. Michael asked me to give you a letter."

Janet blinked. "Michael?"

Chuks nodded, still smiling as he pulled out a small white envelope from his bag. "Yes. He said I should give this to you personally."

He held it out to her.

Janet hesitated, then reached out and took it. Her name was written across the front. What could Michael possibly have to say to her in a letter? To say he liked her or that he didn't like her?

She looked up at Chuks. "Did he say what it's about?"

"Nope. Just told me to make sure you got it." Chuks said and adjusted his bag.

Well, she would read it at home, not now, in the presence of Chuks. "Alright then. Thank you." She said as she made a move to leave.

Chuks stepped slightly in front of her. "Wait. No…he wants you to read it now and reply so I can take your answer back to him."

She blinked. "Now?"

He nodded, already reaching into his school bag again. "Yes. He even gave me another envelope. There's a sheet of paper inside it for your reply."

Well, it couldn't be anything bad if he wanted a reply and even provided a paper and an envelope, she reasoned.

Her hands trembled slightly as she opened the first envelope, the one with her name on it. She unfolded the letter inside, and as her eyes scanned the words, her breath caught.

Eyes wide, she began to read.

*Hello Janet. This is Michael. I know you like me. I like you too. I want you to be my girl. If you accept, please reply, and let us meet at the back of the SS3 block after school tomorrow.*

*What*?! She stared at the words, frozen. For a second, it felt like the world had paused. Then, her heartbeat picked up as she read the message again.

Michael liked her. *Michael!*

A voice inside her said: *Something about this message from him ... feels off.* But what could be off? She wondered.

With her heart thudding, she looked up slowly. "Is this really from Michael?"

Chuks gave her an innocent, confident nod. "Yes, of course."

She searched his face. Nothing mischievous. No smirk, no twitch of guilt. He looked sincere.

She nodded slowly, and took the second envelope from his hand. Inside was a clean blank sheet of white paper.

"Do you have a pen?" He asked, "Or should I give you mine?"

"Bring yours."

He dug into his shirt pocket and handed her a blue plastic pen, with the cap chewed on one end.

With the pen poised, part of her wanted to scream with joy, but another part whispered, *you know this isn't right.*

However, joy was already spreading through her like warm tea on a cold day, and she began to write:

*Yes, I accept. I'll be there. See you tomorrow. Bye.*

Janet folded her note carefully and slid it into the envelope Chuks had given her. Pressing the flap down, she licked the edge of the envelope, and sealed it tight.

Turning to Chuks, she handed it over with a small, grateful smile. "Thank you."

He took it with a quick nod and put it inside his bag.

"Will you give it to him today?" She wanted to know.

Chuks chuckled. "I'll give it to him as soon as I see him."

"Okay. Thanks again."

Janet turned and as she continued her walk home, her mind was no longer on the tests she had to prepare for but on the envelope in her hand.

*Am I really awake or am I dreaming*? She asked herself and glanced around to confirm. The buildings she saw everyday on the road were still there, as well as the street vendors. A female street vendor was shouting something about boiled corn being ready and two younger students walked past, laughing. She looked down at her hand … she was still clutching the envelope.

Yes, she was awake. Very much awake.

A smile crept onto her face. It was small, hesitant at first, then grew wider. She exclaimed. "Wonders shall never end!"

With a skip in her step, she walked the rest of the way home, her heart light; her thoughts racing.

*Michael likes me. He really likes me.*

She almost couldn't wait to get home so she could chat with her three friends and inform them. She knew they would be surprised, but they would also be happy for her.

She reached the house, and the moment she stepped inside the apartment, she kicked off her shoes, and dropped her bag onto the sofa. She brought out the letter from the envelope, and as she read it again, she took in every word with new excitement. Yes, he liked her, and she would be seeing him tomorrow. Her heart felt like it might burst with joy.

She held the letter to her chest and twirled once, giddy. *This is really happening*!

Rereading the letter, some questions began to creep in. *Why the back of the SS3 block?* That place was always quiet…and hidden. *But well, maybe he didn't want other students or teachers to see us talking,* she reasoned.

Another thought popped up. *Why send the letter through Chuks? Why not come to me himself?* She sat down on the sofa and stared at the letter. Maybe…maybe he was shy. That possibility made her smile even more.

*Michael, shy*? It made her like him even more, and her heart did a strange dance in half excitement.

Still grinning and barely able to keep still, she reached for her phone. Opening the WhatsApp group chat she shared with Aanu, Lizzy, and Ada, she typed quickly:

*I have gist for you girls. Tomorrow. BIG gist.*

She added a sly wink emoji, then locked her phone.

At 5pm, she went to the church for choir rehearsal. Her parents met her there straight from work for a brief meeting. Afterward, they all returned home together. Dinner was simple—white rice, red stew, tasty stockfish, and slices of golden fried plantain.

While eating, her parents asked how school was.

"It was okay." She said, forcing herself to sound casual.

"Don't forget you're cleaning the bathroom on Saturday." Her mother added between bites.

"Yes, Mommy."

Later that night, after a warm shower, Janet wore her pink pajamas and crawled into bed. She laid on her stomach, reached under her pillow, and pulled out the letter again. She read it one more time, and then turned onto her back.

Holding the paper against her chest, she stared at the ceiling and began to think about how tomorrow's meeting might go. Would he be waiting there? Would he smile broadly at her? Would he reach out and take her hand? The thought made her giggle.

Her first 'relationship' had just begun. It felt surreal, like something out of the stories they whispered about in class or in novels. *Michael likes me. Me*!

She eventually turned the bedroom light off, but sleep was impossible. She tossed and turned for hours, staring into the darkness with a silly smile on her face.

 **CHAPTER 6**

## The Joke on Janet

By morning, Janet had barely slept, but the excitement she felt more than made up for the exhaustion. She could hardly wait to see her friends.

As soon as she spotted them, she rushed over, eyes sparkling.

"Janet, spill!" Ada demanded before Janet could greet them. "What happened? Don't even say good morning … just start talking!"

Janet laughed, looked around, and then leaned in. "Okay. Are you ready for this?"

"Yes!" Lizzy and Aanu chorused, inching closer.

Janet lowered her voice. "Michael sent me a letter yesterday."

"It's a lie!" Lizzy said and gasped dramatically; mouth open.

"I'm serious." Janet said, grinning.

"Wait. How?" Aanu asked. "When?"

Adjusting the strap of her backpack, Janet explained. "You remember I told you I was going to the library after school yesterday?"

They all nodded eagerly.

"So, when I was coming out of the school gate, Chuks … you know Chuks from Michael's class?"

Her friends nodded.

"He called my name from across the road. He said he was looking for me because Michael gave him a letter to deliver."

"No way!" Ada clutched her chest like someone had dropped a bombshell.

"Wow! So, what did he say?" Lizzy asked, practically bouncing on her toes.

Janet tried to stay composed, but her excitement bubbled out in her voice. "He said … he knows I like him."

"And?" Ada's eyes were wide with anticipation.

"And—" she paused for dramatic effect, her eyes twinkling, "He said he likes me too. Then he asked me to be his girl."

The moment hung in the air for one breathless second. Then the girls let out squeals and gasps of excitement.

"Wow!" Ada squealed, throwing her arms around Janet in an excited hug.

"The letter is here." Janet said, pulling it carefully from her bag.

Aanu snatched it from her gently, her eyes scanning the paper, while Lizzy and Ada practically leaned over her shoulders to read it together. Their eyes widened as they took in each word.

When they finished, Lizzy grabbed the letter and read it again aloud. "'I want you to be my girl.' Wow!"

"I told you!" Aanu said, beaming like a proud aunt. "I told you! Didn't I tell you something might happen?"

"You did." Janet admitted, laughing as she reached out to tug playfully at Aanu's sleeve.

"This is wild." Lizzy muttered, shaking her head. "Wild in the best way."

Ada just stared at Janet; hands clasped like she was witnessing a live romance drama. "So … are you seeing him today?"

Janet nodded shyly, her smile still shining.

Lizzy gave her a sly look. "Hmm. But why does he want to meet you behind the SS3 block?"

Janet shrugged. "I don't know. Maybe he doesn't want anyone seeing us together yet. He might be shy."

"Or maybe he just wants privacy." Aanu teased, raising a brow.

Janet elbowed her. "It's not like that!"

Aanu laughed. "Okay, okay. But just so you know…we won't wait for you after school. You might be…delayed."

The tension and confusion of the previous week melted away as they all burst out laughing.

It felt good—this moment, Janet thought. Like everything had clicked into place.

When they got to school, they headed to their different classrooms.

Janet's heart was dancing as she walked into her class, ready for whatever the day—and Michael—might bring.

She sat through her classes in a daze, the teachers' voices barely registering. Her notebook lay open, pen in hand, but she didn't write much. All she could think about was Michael. *The message. Their plan. Behind the SS3 block. After school.* The words kept repeating in her head.

During break time, she spotted Michael near the canteen. He stood with his usual crowd. He was loud, confident, and laughing at something that one of the boys had said.

A thrill shot through her. *There he is.*

She walked past slowly, trying to appear casual—like she was just heading somewhere. Her steps were steady, but inside, her heart pounded like a drum.

*Maybe he'll look up.* A glance. A smile. A nod. Something from him.

She dared a sidelong glance at him, just a quick one, but Michael didn't even look her way. He didn't acknowledge her at all. His laughter rang out again as though she wasn't even there; as though he hadn't sent any letter to her yesterday.

Janet's chest tightened and she kept walking. Her face was carefully composed, but her thoughts swirled in confusion. He wasn't shy, so why didn't he look at her? Why was he acting like nothing happened?

A thought occurred to her. *Well, maybe he doesn't want his friends to know. Maybe it's all hush-hush for now. That has to be it. He's just being careful.* That explanation offered a bit of comfort, but the uncertainty lingered in her heart.

The rest of the school day crawled like a snail.

By the time the closing bell rang, she was already half out of her seat. She stuffed her books into her bag, slung it over one shoulder, and made her way through the halls, weaving past the crowds of students pouring out into the compound. She wouldn't want to keep Michael waiting.

She eventually reached the back of the SS3 block, but there was no one there. Janet exhaled in relief. *Good*, he hadn't come.

However, the place was quiet—eerily quiet. The chatter and footsteps from the front of the school barely reached there. The back wall was lined with overgrown bushes, and a few broken desks were on the ground.

She leaned against the wall, glancing around, her arms folded.

Soon, one minute passed. Then two. She shifted her weight from one foot to the other, glancing at the path leading from the school building.

Another minute passed. Still no one. *Maybe he's just running late. He'll come. He has to come,* she reasoned, trying to steady her nerves. And she hoped he would come soon as she wouldn't want to be here alone for too long.

She looked again at the low shrubs behind her. *I hope there aren't any snakes in there*, she thought with a grimace.

Another minute ticked by. As she checked the time on her phone, her ears strained for footsteps. Voices. Something. But there was nothing.

Still, she stayed. Waiting.

Suddenly, she heard footsteps from the other side of the building.

*At last*! With her heart leaping, she turned in the direction, with a small smile.

But it wasn't Michael. She saw four boys approaching her. Her heart dropped as she recognized them immediately—Tunde, Chuks, and two of their friends.

They were grinning. Too widely.

Janet stiffened.

"Hey!" Tunde called out, the mischief already in his voice. "Did you get Michael's letter?"

Her mind raced. "Yes." She said slowly, her voice uncertain.

*Did Michael send them? Is he coming behind them?*

She didn't have to wonder long as the boys burst into laughter.

Tunde took a step closer, still laughing. "You actually believed it?"

Janet blinked, confused. "What do you mean?"

"I wrote it." Tunde said proudly, as if he'd just pulled off the greatest prank in the world.

The laughter from the boys got louder.

Her breath caught. "What?!"

"It was a joke!" Another boy added, slapping Tunde's back. "And you fell for it so fast!"

Janet's mouth fell open. She wanted to talk but the words wouldn't come.

"She really liked Michael." One of them snickered. "She really thought she had a chance."

"She even said yes!" Tunde added, mimicking a high-pitched voice. "'*Yes, I accept. I'll be there.*'"

Their laughter exploded again.

What was their plan? She wondered … outnumbered. Humiliated.

Suddenly very aware that she was alone with them, she began to back away, her hands curling around the strap of her backpack.

"Don't go now." One of the boys teased, holding out his arms. "Come on!"

"Michael's girl!" Chuks jeered.

She turned sharply, and ran.

Her legs moved on instinct as she sprinted toward the front of the school. She didn't look back. And she didn't stop running until she reached the school gate, where some students were still hanging around. She slowed down to catch her breath.

But Tunde and his friends weren't done. They came out a few minutes later, still laughing and joking loudly about the prank.

They spotted her near the gate and didn't hold back. "That's the girl! She thought Michael liked her!"

A few other students looked their way, curious.

"She actually said yes!" Chuks added, laughing hard.

More laughter followed as they pointed at her.

 # CHAPTER 7

## Tears Behind the Door

Janet kept walking, almost wishing that the ground would open up and swallow her. Soon, the voices and laughter behind her faded, but the sting of what happened remained, still very painful.

The faces of passersby blurred as she kept her eyes down, not wanting to meet anyone's gaze. A lone tear rolled down her cheek, but she brushed it away. Not now. She should wait until she got home, she told herself.

She walked home alone in silence, her legs heavy, her heart aching. She finally reached her street and, even though some dogs were barking, she hardly noticed. She just wanted to get inside her apartment and shut the door behind her.

Soon, she got to the apartment, fumbled with the key, and opened the door. Once inside, she slammed it shut and locked it. Dropping her backpack with a thud, she collapsed on the sofa and began to weep. Huge, heaving sobs shook her small frame. The shame, the betrayal, the public humiliation—it was too much. She had never experienced anything like that before.

When her weeping subsided, the images of what happened began to play on repeat in her mind—the sneers, the laughter, the look on Tunde's face. *He planned it. He wanted to humiliate me.*

Was Michael involved? Did he know about this?! She wondered. Even if he wasn't involved, he would hear about it, she was certain. If he hadn't already.

*How could they do this to me*? She whispered into the quiet with tears streaming down her cheeks. And more importantly, *why did this happen to me? What did I ever do to deserve this?*

The image of Tunde and his friends laughing, the mockery at the school gate, the whispers and shocked stares of the other students…all of it began to replay in her mind on an endless loop.

*How am I supposed to face the students tomorrow? Or Tunde and his friends? And the students by the gate who heard Tunde and his friends.*

She sat up suddenly, wiping her face roughly with the back of her hand. "No." She said aloud, her voice shaky but firm. "I can't do this! I can't go back there!"

An abrupt thought occurred to her … *maybe I should just commit suicide and end it all. That way, I won't have to face any of the students*. The gossip. The shame. Her problems … they would all be over.

She knew that this thought about suicide was of the devil, but she was tempted to consider it.

*Should I do it?* Then she remembered something … two months ago, during one of the teen sessions at church, a youth leader had spoken on suicide. His voice came back clearly now.

"Suicide is a lie from the devil." He'd said. "It's never the solution, and should not even be an option. It's a trick of the devil to cut a life short before God's purpose is fulfilled. No matter what you are going through or how deep the pain, there is hope in Christ. He will help you."

As Janet continued thinking about it, she shook her head slowly and said, "No. I don't want to die. I really don't. I have a lot to live for."

Just as suddenly as the evil voice spoke to her mind, another voice rose within her … *Don't commit suicide.*

*You shouldn't. God loves you. He cares. He can help you through this.*

Staring at the wall, she asked herself, *how did I even get into this mess? I'm a Christian; I believe in God.* Questions filled her heart, but there were no answers. Only silence.

She knew she should pray at this point so she could make the right decision, but her heart felt too heavy to do so.

She eventually decided that she would not go to school the next day. "I can't."

But then, another question came to her mind: *What excuse will you give your parents for wanting to stay away from school? And for how long can you stay away from school?*

She didn't know. All she knew was that she didn't want to face anyone. Not the boys. Not Michael. Not even her friends. Not after what had just happened.

Her phone began to ring suddenly, startling her. She wiped her wet cheeks, took the phone, and checked the screen. It was Lizzy.

She dropped the phone. *I can't talk. Not now.*

About two minutes after, she received a chat from Lizzy.

*Hey babe! Soooo? How did it go with Michael? Don't keep us in suspense!*

Janet didn't reply.

After a while, she stood. Dragging herself to her room, she changed out of her school uniform with sluggish movements.

She went to the kitchen to get food and, as she ate, the food tasted like sawdust in her mouth.

There was church service that evening, and usually, she would have gone without hesitation. But today? She didn't want to go; she couldn't pretend that everything was fine. Deciding not to attend, she sent a message to her mother to explain that she needed to rest.

Afterward, she messaged her friends, telling them everything—every cruel word, every mocking laugh, everything Tunde and his friends had done.

*Tunde and his friends set me up. It was all a joke ... Everything. The letter, the meeting, everything ...*

They called her almost immediately.

"What?" Lizzy shouted through the phone. "He actually did that? Are you serious right now?!"

"Yes." She sniffed and wiped her face with the back of her hand.

"I can't believe it." Aanu added, her voice full of fury. "That guy has some nerve! Who does that kind of thing?! That's not even funny. That's wickedness!"

"I don't think I can show my face in school tomorrow." Janet said quietly. "I just … I can't. I feel so stupid" As she talked with them, she was sniffing.

"I feel like punching Tunde right now." Aanu growled. "He needs to be confronted. He cannot get away with this."

In bed at night, Janet cried quietly into her pillow. She decided she would lie and tell her parents in the morning that she had a headache or was not feeling well and would not be able to go to school.

She closed her eyes, hoping to sleep soon, but sleep didn't come easily. When it eventually did, it was light and troubled.

When she woke up in the morning, she groaned and turned on her side as sunlight peeked through the curtains. Her head throbbed. *Great. Now I actually have a headache.*

She got out of bed slowly and dragged herself into the living room where her parents were finishing their breakfast.

"Mom?" Her voice came out weak and uncertain.

Her mother looked up immediately. "Janet, what's wrong?"

"I … I don't feel well." She said, with a hand pressed to her head for emphasis. "I have a really bad headache. I don't think I can go to school today."

Her father lowered his phone. "Did this just start this morning?"

"Yes, kind of. It started late last night. I was tossing all night."

Her mother stood and walked over, placing the back of her hand on Janet's neck. "Hmm. You don't have a fever."

"I know, but my head really hurts." Janet murmured, trying to sound as tired as she felt emotionally.

Her mother sighed, clearly unconvinced but also concerned. "Okay. After breakfast, take a pain reliever and try to rest. I'll pray for you now."

She took Janet's hands and prayed, asking God for healing, peace of mind, and strength.

This made Janet feel worse. She felt guilty for lying, and she asked God for forgiveness.

After her parents left for work, Janet returned to her room. She sat on the edge of her bed, staring at the floor.

*How am I going to face them?* The students, Michael … Tunde and his friends?! Her stomach twisted.

Then her eyes widened. *Tomorrow is Friday. Oh no*! She would have to go to school tomorrow as the school fellowship would be having a guest minister, and she was the one that would lead the praise and worship. Would the students who have heard what happened want to listen to her sing and pray? She doubted it.

*What if they laugh? What if no one takes me seriously anymore?* She loved to sing; it brought her joy, but now it felt like she had ruined things for herself, and it was being taken away from her.

She buried her face in her hands. What could she do about tomorrow? Should she call and tell the fellowship coordinators that she wouldn't be able to sing? Would they even understand?

She realized it might be too late to say she would not be able to sing tomorrow. Feeling troubled and confused, she decided to pray.

She slid to her knees beside her bed and began, "God, I don't even know what to say. I feel so bad. Please help me."

Her voice cracked and she paused to wipe her tears. After some time in prayer, she stood, went to the kitchen to eat something light, took the pain reliever, and crawled back into bed.

 # CHAPTER 8

## Whispers of Hope

On Friday morning, Janet left the house for school. She met up with her friends, and on the way, Aanu said, "We told him."

Janet blinked. "Told who?"

"Tunde. Yesterday, after school. We confronted him. We told him off … big time."

"We couldn't let him get away with that nonsense." Lizzy said, her eyes flashing. "We told him what he did was disgusting."

The news did little to change how Janet was feeling, but she thanked them.

Many students would have heard about it. And Michael. And Chioma.

She could only hope that the fellowship teachers would not know. They would certainly not be happy with her. One of them even attended her church. If the teacher should tell her parents, she knew that she would be in serious trouble. The thought alone made her stomach churn.

At school, she walked straight to her class, head low. During break, she remained seated, pretending to be absorbed in her notes. Laughter rang out from a group near the window, and though she didn't turn to look, she felt that it was about her.

Still, she kept her eyes on her desk, refusing to look in their direction or cry.

When school ended, she made her way to the school fellowship venue. *Please, Lord. Help me, in Jesus' name.* She kept repeating under her breath.

The fellowship began with someone leading the opening prayer. When eventually her name was called, her heart pounded in her chest. She stepped forward and collected the microphone, gripping it tightly.

She closed her eyes and began to sing. Her voice trembled at first, but soon, she felt better, and her voice grew steady and confident. The students sang along.

When she finished and returned to her seat, she closed her eyes and said, "Thank You, Lord."

She wasn't sure what would come next, but for the first time since everything happened, she felt like she had taken one step forward.

Soon, the guest minister was introduced and it was time to listen to the message.

Janet brought out her pen and notebook, ready to take notes as she had been taught in church.

The woman, Pastor Jane, prayed and said she would want someone to read the scripture, Romans 12:1-2.

A boy stood with his Bible and began to read the New King James Version. ***"I beseech you therefore, brethren, by the mercies of God, that you present your bodies a living sacrifice, holy, acceptable to God, which is your reasonable service. And do not be conformed to this world, but be transformed by the renewing of your mind, that you may prove what is that good and acceptable and perfect will of God."***

Pastor Jane went on. "How many of you have done something just because everyone else is doing it? And sometimes, deep down in your heart you know that it's not right? How many of you have experienced it?"

She paused and glanced around.

Some students raised their hands … some hesitantly; others without shame as whispered murmurs passed through rows of chairs.

Janet sat still. She didn't raise her hand, but her heart did. *That's me,* she thought, pressing her lips together. *She's talking about me.*

The pastor nodded. "I see those hands. Thank you for being honest. Yes, we've all been there. And that's peer pressure for those who might not understand what it is. It is when you want to do things just to fit in. Wanting to be liked. Peer pressure makes a person go in the opposite direction of God's will. It pulls you…sometimes in a subtle way, sometimes forcefully…away from what you know is right. Away from God's will."

Janet lowered her gaze as her mind drifted immediately to her friends and everything that had happened with Michael, with Tunde, and with the setup. She had gone along with things that she shouldn't have; laughed at things she didn't believe in; and stayed quiet when she should've spoken up…all to belong.

The pastor continued, "It's something that teenagers face a lot, and I've decided to talk to you about *How to stand strong when the crowd pulls.*"

Picking up her Bible, she flipped to Daniel chapter one. "Let's look at a young man called Daniel. He was young when he was taken to Babylon. He was surrounded by a new culture, new expectations, but listen to what verse 8 says: 'Daniel purposed in his heart that he would not defile himself.'"

She paused and repeated it slowly. "He purposed in his heart. That means he decided…he drew a line. Even though everyone around him was doing the wrong thing, Daniel stood firm."

Janet swallowed hard as she thought … *Daniel decided. I didn't. I followed the crowd.* She realized that she should have run away from the bad influence of Aanu, Lizzy, and Ada, and kept running.

Pastor Jane went on. "You see, God honored Daniel's decision and gave him wisdom, understanding, and influence. This is because God blesses those who honor Him!"

Some teachers and students nodded in understanding, as the hall grew quieter.

"Now," she continued, "why do people give in to peer pressure? Let me tell you some reasons. Number one: fear of rejection. Number two: low self-esteem."

As she mentioned them, Janet could relate.

"Don't allow yourself to be pulled by the wrong crowd." She said firmly.

Janet took a deep breath, knowing she had allowed herself to be pulled by the wrong crowd.

"God does not want you to follow the crowd; He wants you to follow Jesus." The pastor pointed out. "Allowing yourself to be pulled can lead to years of regret; of consequences. But that is not God's will for you. God's plans for you are good, not evil. He wants to give you the expected end."

Janet took a deep breath again.

The pastor continued. "In order to do what is right, you have to be strong and remain strong. And to be strong, you have to draw your strength from God. The Bible says—be strong in the Lord and in the power of His might. Not your own strength, but God's strength."

She explained the scripture, and then she began to talk about how to be strong and resist peer pressure. "Let me give you practical steps. Number one: Know what the Bible says. Don't just guess; know the truth, and stand on the truth. The Bible says, ***You shall know the truth, and the truth shall set you free***."

She continued mentioning the points, and then looking directly at a section of the hall, she said, "Number five, to stand strong, you need godly friends. The Bible says … he ***that walks with the wise shall be wise, but the companion of fools shall be destroyed***. You can't stand strong if your friends or the people closest to you are the ones leading you into weakness. You can't say no to sin when your friends say yes to it every day. To be strong, choose friends who draw you closer to God."

Janet breathed in deeply again as she realized it was time to make a change. She couldn't keep sinning or trying to be someone she wasn't, just to belong. And she couldn't keep pretending that she was still a good Christian. It was time to walk away from the wrong crowd, she told herself.

The pastor also talked about the power of prayer.

As she continued speaking to the group, her words seemed to pierce through the haze in Janet's mind, and she shifted slightly on her seat. The pastor wasn't just preaching; she was touching Janet's heart.

*Maybe I should talk to her. Maybe she could help me figure this mess out—Michael, Tunde, my so-called friends...all of it*, Janet thought. Something about the woman's calm, firm voice made Janet feel like she would be understood and counseled properly.

When the talk ended, Pastor Jane led a brief prayer, and as she put the microphone down, everyone clapped in appreciation.

She returned to her seat while someone from the organizing team stepped forward.

The person appreciated the woman for coming, and then announced, "If anyone would like to see Pastor Jane for counseling, you're welcome to come forward now."

Immediately, three students got up and made their way to the front. Pastor Jane moved to a seat at the side and gestured for the first girl to sit across from her. The remaining two sat a few chairs away, waiting their turn.

 CHAPTER 9

## More Than Your Mistakes

Janet hesitated as her heart thudded against her ribs. *Just go before you change your mind,* she counseled herself.

She stood up abruptly and walked to join the two students, avoiding eye contact with anyone in the room.

When it was finally her turn, she sat across from Pastor Jane.

The woman gave her a warm, reassuring smile. "You wanted to talk?" She asked gently.

Janet nodded, her hands twisting in her lap. "Yes, Ma. I ... I don't even know where to start."

"Start wherever you feel comfortable." Pastor Jane said, still smiling.

So, Janet began. She talked about her three friends and how she had found herself doing things that were not quite right and things that she wasn't ready for.

Her voice trembled, but she continued. She explained about how she had started thinking about Michael and how she agreed to be in a relationship with him, not realizing that the letter was written by Tunde. And how Tunde and his friends had humiliated her and how her friends said they confronted Tunde.

"I've made such a mess, Ma." She said at last, tears threatening at the corners of her eyes. "And I've been crying since. What can I do?"

Pastor Jane leaned forward slightly. "First of all, I'm glad you came to talk to me. It's a big step to open up like this."

Janet nodded; eyes lowered.

"I know that facing these people and all these emotions must feel really tough for you right now," Pastor Jane continued, "but, I want you to know something—this situation does not define you. However, you're still young. This is the time to discover who you are in God, and not to be wrapped up in romantic relationships or accept any boy's proposal."

Janet looked up slowly, listening closely.

"Getting into those things too early can cloud your judgment. It can cause confusion, pain, and distractions that you're not emotionally equipped to handle yet. Look at what has happened to you … how it has affected you … the tears and the heartache. This pain wouldn't have come if you hadn't accepted the proposal. I'm not saying this to shame you, but to help you see clearly." Pastor Jane said. "Do you understand?"

Janet gave a small nod. "I understand." She whispered. "I know all these things … but I don't know how I allowed everything to happen. Maybe I … I was just trying to belong."

Pastor Jane gave her a compassionate look. "You already belong to Jesus. He understands you, and wants so much more for you than this temporary attention from people who don't even understand you the right way or understand God's purpose for your life. The girls you call your friends and those boys are also young, and if they don't know much about God, there's no way they can do things right or give you the right advice. The influence and advice of those three girls led you down the wrong path."

Janet nodded in understanding.

"Now, I want to talk to you about how you handled your feelings. Or rather, how you should have handled them."

Janet nodded silently.

"Just because you like a boy doesn't mean it's the right time to start a relationship. You're supposed to pray about it and seek guidance from a godly adult—preferably a woman since you're a young woman—who can counsel you on how to manage your emotions wisely."

Janet nodded again.

Pastor Jane continued, "Whenever you're unsure about whether something is right or wrong, ask yourself this question: What would my pastor say if he or she heard about this? Think about it. If your pastor would not be pleased, then it's a clear sign that it's not the right thing to do."

Janet nodded in understanding.

The woman continued, "You can also ask yourself, 'What would Jesus do?' If Jesus wouldn't do it, then you shouldn't either. It's really that simple."

There was a pause, then she asked pointedly, "Tell me, what do you think your pastor would say if he heard you were in a relationship at this stage of your life?"

Janet swallowed hard. "He wouldn't be happy." She admitted in almost a whisper.

"Exactly. And your parents? You said that your parents are Christians."

Janet nodded.

"They would also not be pleased. That alone should help you know that the time is not right. Right now, your focus should be on your education. But, more importantly, on knowing who you are in Christ and growing deeper in Him. Relationships will come later at the right time. And because you're a Christian, God Himself will lead you to one of His sons—a man who will truly value and appreciate you."

"Okay."

"Do you understand?"

Janet nodded again, this time more slowly. "Yes, but…what about the embarrassment? What should I do? Everyone knows; I feel so ashamed."

The woman gave a soft sigh, then placed a comforting hand on her shoulder. "Take that to God in prayer. He sees your heart. He knows the pain you're feeling; He cares for you deeply. He can, and He will heal your emotions. Alright?"

Janet nodded.

"You will be fine." She assured Janet.

Janet nodded again.

Pastor Jane sat back. "Let's pray now."

Janet hesitated for a second, then closed her eyes.

"Tell God how you feel." The woman said. "Say it. Say, 'Lord, I feel ashamed. I feel hurt, but I bring it to You.' Go on."

Janet took a deep breath and repeated the words with trembling lips. "Lord, I feel ashamed. I feel hurt … but I bring it to You in Jesus' Name."

"Good." The woman encouraged. "Now ask Him to heal your heart … and to help you forgive anyone who has hurt you. Also, ask for strength to walk confidently in Him again, and pray that this situation turns around for your good … in Jesus' Name."

As Janet prayed, her voice broke and tears streamed down her cheeks. She didn't try to stop them; she just let them fall.

When she finished, the woman placed her hand on her head and prayed for her, declaring peace, healing, and restoration.

Then she looked into Janet's eyes and said, "God cares for you, but let this be a lesson. Stay away from relationships until the time is right."

"Yes, Ma."

"Now, whenever you have time today, I'd like you to read and meditate on a few scriptures."

Janet immediately reached into her bag and pulled out a pen and paper.

"Write these down." The woman said. "Proverbs 4:23; Ecclesiastes 3:1; Isaiah 41:10; 2Timothy 2:22."

She paused and added three more scriptures.

Janet wrote each one carefully.

"Good. Keep praying, and put the past behind you, Janet. Don't let it define who you are."

Janet nodded slowly.

"Above all," Pastor Jane continued, "don't stop being a Christian in your school. Let your light shine even brighter now. This is the time to stand out. You hear me?"

"Yes, Ma." Janet answered.

"Good. It is well with you in Jesus' name."

"Amen. Thank you, Ma." Janet said with genuine gratitude.

Pastor Jane smiled and patted her hand. "You're welcome. Also, you should be able to talk to your parents especially your mom whenever there's a challenge. Don't keep things bottled up. Talk to your parents … or your pastor or his wife. I know your pastor and his wife; they are good people. They'll listen."

"Yes, Ma." Janet replied.

Janet thanked her again and as she got up, she realized that she felt a lot better.

She didn't see any of the three girls around, and she headed for the gate.

Outside the gate, she looked around, and spotted Chioma at the roadside, handing money to a corn vendor.

"Chioma!" Janet called out.

Chioma turned, surprised. "Janet!" Her eyes lit up with a smile.

She walked up to Chioma and noticed the small plastic bag in Chioma's hand. "Five corns? Are you planning to start a corn business?" She teased.

Chioma laughed. "Please! My grandma likes corn and asked me to buy them."

"Oh, I see." Janet said as they started walking together.

At home in the evening, Janet sat cross-legged on her bed. With her Bible in her hand, she turned to each scripture Pastor Jane had given her. She read slowly, whispering each word, so they could sink in like medicine to her soul.

As she meditated on the scriptures, a deep sense of conviction came over her, and everything became clearer. She thought about how far she had strayed since she started following the three girls … the lies she had told her parents, the choices she had made, the boy she had almost given her heart to, and the girls she had followed. What if Tunde and his friends had taken advantage of her behind that building? Who would have saved her? She shuddered. It was God who saved her, she knew.

Tears welled up again, but this time, they were tears of gratitude, and she whispered, "Thank You, Lord."

That night, she made a firm decision in her heart—to change. She would like to have a closer walk with God, and be more intentional about the friends she kept.

Chioma came to her mind … her calm spirit, and her quiet strength. She truly loved the Lord and was living to please Him. That was the kind of friend she needed.

*I'll draw closer to the students who are serious with God; especially Chioma*, she resolved. No more compromises.

She knelt by her bed and began to pray, "Thank You, Lord … for everything."

# QUESTIONS

1. How would people usually describe Janet's personality? And how do you think others would describe your personality?

2. What made Janet first keep her distance from Aanu, Lizzy, and Ada?

3. Why did Janet look back before talking to her friends?
A) She was looking for Michael.
B) She wanted to make sure no student could hear her.
C) She wanted to see if her parents were coming.
D) She was feeling shy.

4. How would you feel if someone found out a secret you told only to your close friends?

5. Do you think Aanu's apology was sincere? Why or why not?

6. Should friends be allowed to share each other's secrets with their other friends? Why or why not?

7. Janet's three friends misled her after she confided in them about her feelings for Michael. Do you think they did this intentionally? If not, what do you think caused it?

8. What should Janet have done differently when she first realized her feelings for Michael?

9. Should Janet have taken more time to think before writing a reply to the letter? Why or why not?

10. Do you believe Michael really wrote the letter? What clues support your opinion?

11. Do you think what the boys did was harmless fun or a form of bullying? Explain your answer.

12. Have you ever felt hopeless or overwhelmed like Janet? Who or what helped you get through it?

13. What does it mean to 'purpose in your heart' like Daniel did? What decision can you make today to live with more purpose and integrity?

14. Suicide is never the solution, and should not even be an option. What do you think this statement means?

# ALSO BY TAIWO IREDELE ODUBIYI

## Christian fiction for adults

*In Love for Us  
*Love Fever  
*Love on the Pulpit  
*Shadows from the Past  
*This Time Around  
*Oh Baby!  
*Tears on My Pillow  
*To Love Again  
*You Found Me  
*My First Love  
*With This Ring  
*The Forever Kind of Love  
*What Changed You?  
*Too Much of a Good Thing  
*Is it Me You're Looking for?  
*Marriage on Fire  
*Then Came You  
*The One for Me  
*Sea of Regrets  
*Shipwrecked With You  
*Life Goes On  
*I'll Take You There  
*My Desire  
*If You Could See Me Now  
*Never Say Never!

*When A Man Loves a Woman

*Christmas to Remember        *Accidentally Yours

*She Who Has a Man        *Comfort and Joy

*Broken Together        *Friends to Forever

*One Day in December        *Made a Way

*To have and to hold        *Christmas Joy


**Novel for teenagers**

A Brother's Promise


**Storybooks for Children**

*Rescued by Victor        *No One is a Nobody

*The Boy Who Stole

*Joe and His Stepmother, Bibi

*Nike & the Stranger        *Billy the Bully

*Greater Tomorrow

*Jonah's First Day of School

*Bimbo Learns a Lesson

**Nonfiction for adults**

*30 Things Husbands Do That Hurt Their Wives

*30 Things Wives Do That Hurt Their Husbands

*Rape & How to Handle it

*Divine Instructions to live by – 1

*God's Words to Singles

*God's Words to Couples

*God's Words to Older Adults

*Real Answers, Real Quick! (for singles)

*Real Answers, Real Quick! (for couples)

*God's Words to Women in Ministry

*6 Hard Truths About Marriage & How to Handle Them

*Fixing mistakes & Bad decisions

# About the Author

Taiwo Iredele Odubiyi is a pastor and the Executive President of TenderHearts Family Support Initiative, a Non-Governmental Organization, and Pastor Taiwo Odubiyi Ministries. She has a deep and strong passion for relationships and expresses this in ministries - nationally and internationally - to children, teenagers, singles, women and couples. She reaches out to these groups through counseling, seminars and programs such as Tenderheartslink, an online program for Christian singles and couples. Married and blessed with children, she is the host of the YouTube channel – Tenderheartslink!

I love hearing from the readers of my books. If this book has blessed you, please send your comments to:
Tel: +1(410)220-5676
WhatsApp: +234(802)300-0773

Facebook: Pastor Mrs. Taiwo Odubiyi

Twitter: @pastortaiwoodub

Instagram: @pastortaiwoiredeleodubiyi


If you have friends and loved ones, then you do have people you should bless with copies of these very interesting and life-changing novels and books!